# Eject

## Dee Phillips

# RiGHT NOW!

| | |
|---|---|
| Blast | Goal |
| Dare | Goodbye |
| Dumped | Grind |
| **Eject** | Joyride |
| Fight | Mirror |
| Friends? | Scout |

First published by Evans Brothers Limited

2A Portman Mansions, Chiltern Street, London W1U 6NR, United Kingdom

Copyright © Ruby Tuesday Books Limited 2010

This edition published under license from Evans Limited

All rights reserved

**SADDLEBACK**
EDUCATIONAL PUBLISHING
www.sdlback.com

ISBN-13: 978-1-62250-881-5
ISBN-10: 1-62250-881-5
eBook: 978-1-63078-016-6

Printed in Malaysia

20 19 18 17 16    2 3 4 5 6

Suddenly we saw a missile.
It was heading straight for us.
A heat-seeking missile!
We were under attack.

Eject Eject Eject

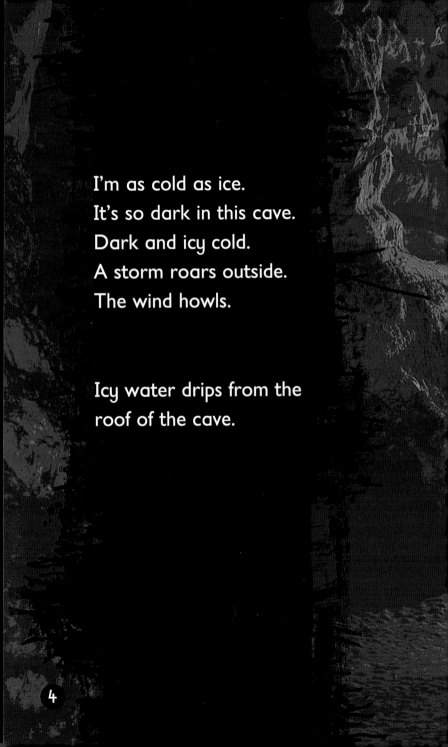

I'm as cold as ice.
It's so dark in this cave.
Dark and icy cold.
A storm roars outside.
The wind howls.

Icy water drips from the
roof of the cave.

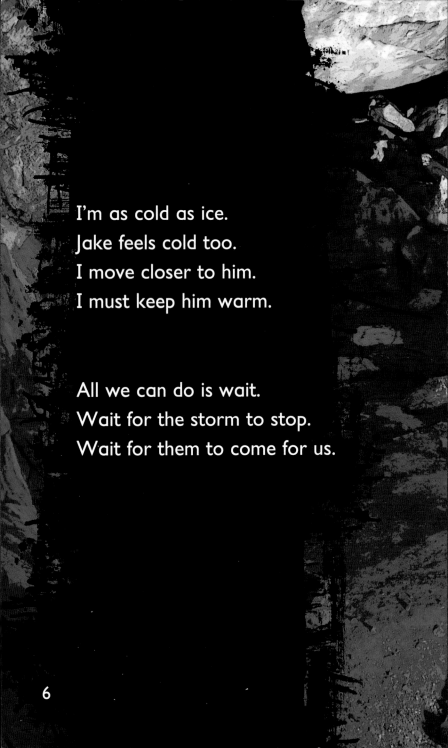

I'm as cold as ice.
Jake feels cold too.
I move closer to him.
I must keep him warm.

All we can do is wait.
Wait for the storm to stop.
Wait for them to come for us.

Jake moans in pain.
His legs are broken.

I say, "We'll be OK, man."

I say, "We'll soon be back
on base. I'll buy you a drink
when we get there."

All we can do is wait ...

We were on a mission.
I was in the pilot's seat.
Jake was the navigator.

WE WERE FLYING LOW.
LOW AND FAST.

Suddenly we saw a missile.
It was heading straight for us.
A heat-seeking missile!
We were under attack.

I broke left.

# I broke right.

I tried to shake off the missile.
But it was still heading
straight for us.

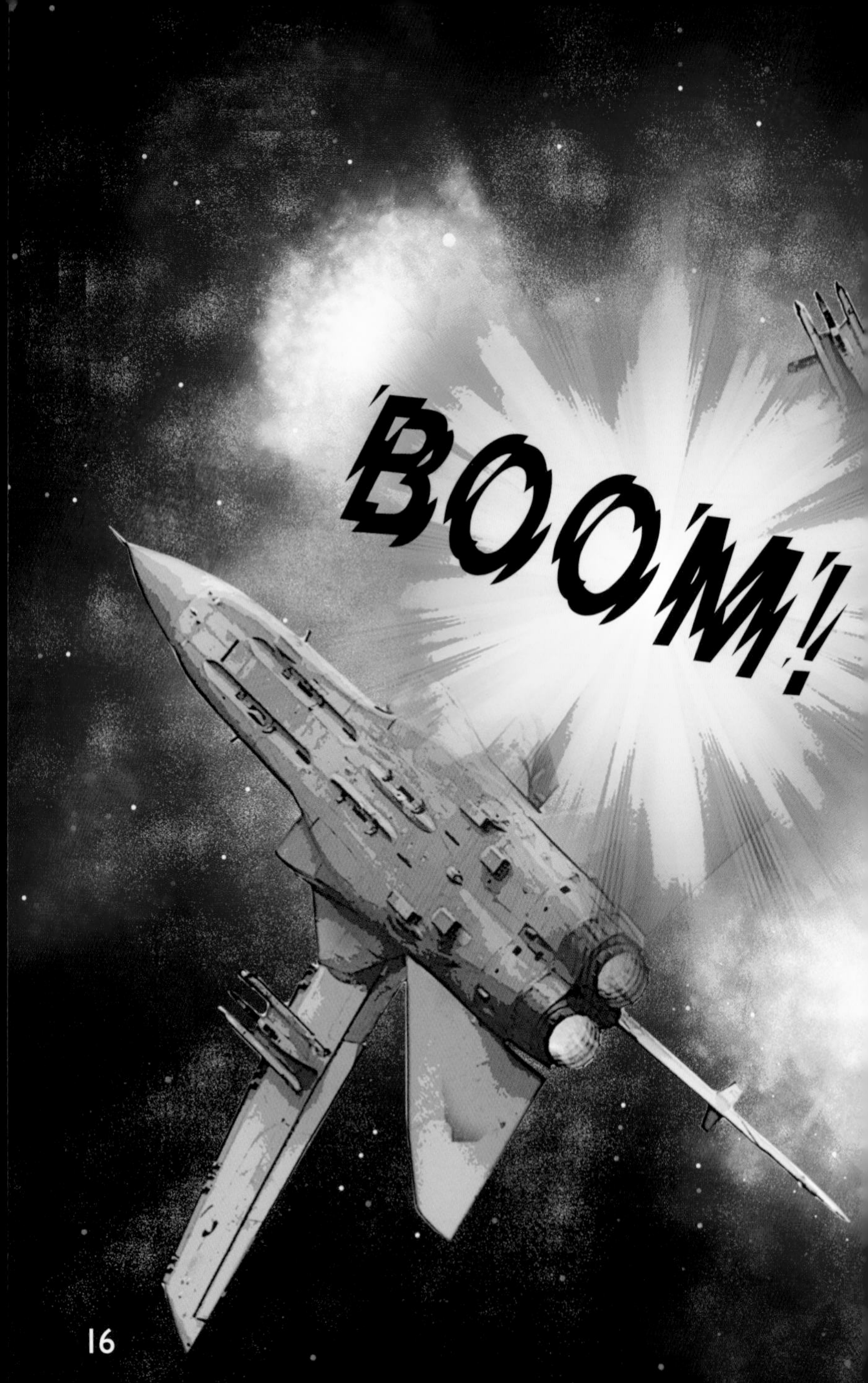
BOOM!

The missile hit us.

We lost our left wing.

We were spinning.

We were falling.

We were burning up.

# Spinning
# Falling
# Burning

We had to get out.

I shouted,

"Eject

Eject

Eject."

I pulled the eject handle.
Straps pulled tight on my arms and legs.

# BOOM!
The plane's
canopy blew off.

# BANG!
I shot out
of the plane.

I flew into the air
like a rocket.

21

I'm as cold as ice.
It's so dark in this cave.
Dark and icy cold.
Jake feels very cold.
I must keep him warm.
He's in a lot of pain.

I say, "We'll be OK, man."

Icy water drips from the
roof of the cave.

I am so cold.
So cold and tired.
I want to sleep.
But I must stay awake
for Jake.

All we can do is wait.
They will come soon.
They will come when
the storm stops.

After I ejected, my parachute opened.

I floated down.

Everything was quiet.

But where were the enemy fighters?

Where was Jake?

# I hit the ground hard!

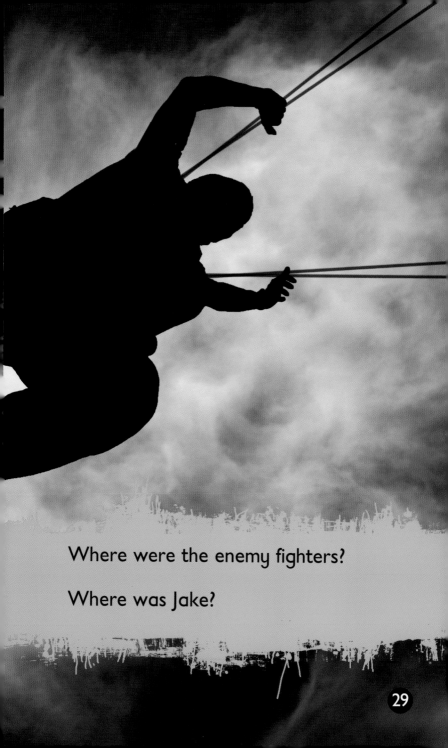

Where were the enemy fighters?

Where was Jake?

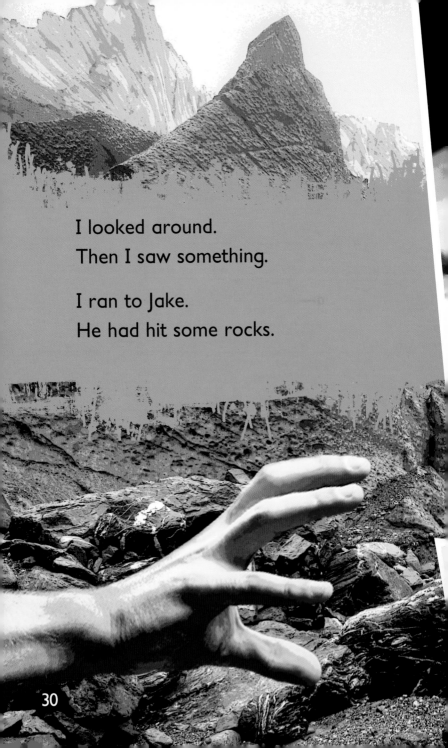

I looked around.
Then I saw something.

I ran to Jake.
He had hit some rocks.

He said, "Help me, Eric."
I said, "You'll be OK, man."

His legs were broken.
His head was bleeding. 31

I radioed the base.

I said, "We're in
trouble. How soon
can you get here?"

There was
a problem.
A big problem.

A huge storm was heading straight for us.

The rescue helicopter could not fly
in the storm.

There was another problem.
I could see the enemy fighters.
They were about a mile away.

We had to hide.

If they found us, they would kill us.

I saw this cave.

I pulled Jake into it.

We waited inside the cave.
Outside, we could hear shouting.

The shouting got closer
and closer.

Jake was moaning.

I said, "Keep quiet, man."

Then the storm hit.

37

It's morning.
It is light outside.
Suddenly we hear voices.

The voices get closer
and closer.

We wait.

# It's our guys!

A soldier says, "It's good to see you guys."
Another says, "We're taking you both home!"

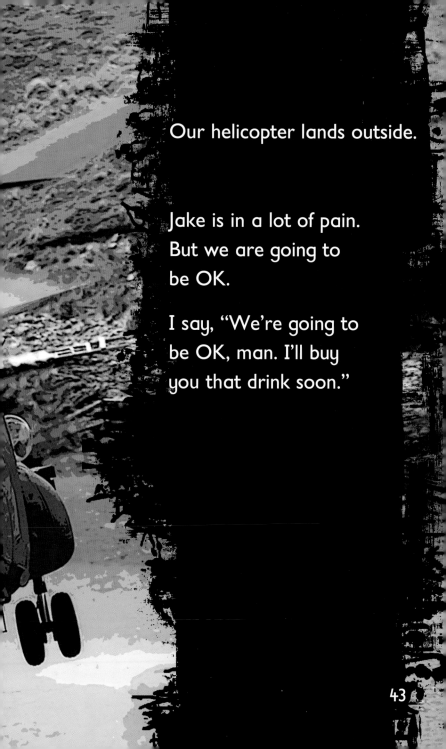

Our helicopter lands outside.

Jake is in a lot of pain.
But we are going to
be OK.

I say, "We're going to
be OK, man. I'll buy
you that drink soon."

## TORNADOES
### ON YOUR OWN

The fighter jet in this book is a Tornado. It's used in NATO and UN military operations. Find out more facts about this plane online.

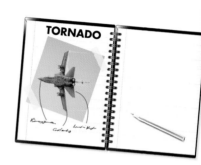

Draw a diagram or use a photograph of a Tornado to create a fact file about the plane.

## MEET UP
### WITH A PARTNER

Imagine that the pilots, Eric and Jake, meet up back on the base. It's a few weeks after the crash, and Jake is in a wheelchair. Eric buys Jake that drink he promised him!

- Discuss how each character would feel.
- Discuss what they would talk about.
- Role-play the conversation that the two characters have.

# SURVIVORS
## IN A GROUP

Your plane has crashed in the mountains. A storm is coming. You need to find shelter. You don't know when you will be rescued.

- As a group, choose the ten most useful items from the plane that will help you survive.
- Rank your items in order of importance.
- Time yourselves. Can you make a decision in under 30 minutes?

# FiGHTER PiLOT
## ON YOUR OWN / WITH A PARTNER / IN A GROUP

Eric's job is to attack enemy aircraft in the air or to bomb enemies on the ground. It took him four years to train as a fighter pilot.

- What kind of person would make a good fighter pilot? Make a list of words to describe them.
- Look online. What skills do fighter pilots need to learn? Make a list of these.
- Make a poster advertising fighter pilot training.
- Role-play an interview for fighter pilot training school.

HAVE YOU GOT WHAT IT TAKES?

IF YOU ENJOYED
THIS BOOK,
TRY THESE OTHER
**RiGHT NOW!**
BOOKS.

Laci and Jaden were in love, but now it's over. So why is Jaden always watching her?

Alisha's online messages to new girl Sam get nastier and nastier. Will anyone help Sam?

Will hates what he sees in the mirror. Brenna does too. Their lives would be so much better if they looked different.

FIGHT

It's Saturday night.
Two angry guys. Two knives.
There's going to be a fight.

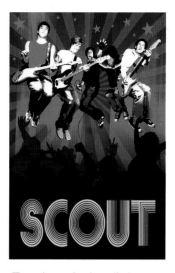

SCOUT

Tonight is the band's big
chance. Tonight, a record
company scout is at their gig!

BLAST

Damien's platoon is under
attack. Another soldier is in
danger. Damien must risk his
own life to save him.

DARE

It's just an old, empty house.
Kristi must spend the night
inside. Just Kristi and
the ghost …

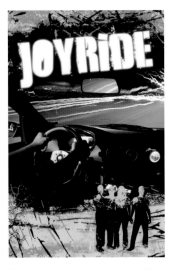

**JOYRIDE**

Tanner sees the red car. The keys are inside. Tanner says to Jacob, Bailey, and Hannah, "Want to go for a drive?"

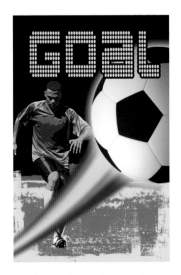

**GOAL**

Today is Carlos's tryout with Chivas. There's just one place up for grabs. But today, everything is going wrong!

**GRIND**

Taylor hates this new town. She misses her friends. There's nowhere to skate!

**DUMPED**

Tonight, Kayla must make a choice. Stay in Philadelphia with her boyfriend, Ryan. Or start a new life in California.